THE EMPEROR'S NEW CLOTHES

Once upon a time there lived a vain emperor whose only worry in life was to dress in elegant clothes. He changed clothes almost every hour, and loved to show them off to his people.

Word of the emperor's grandeur spread through his kingdom and beyond. Hearing of the emperor's vanity, two scoundrels decided to take advantage of it. They presented themselves at the palace gates.

"We are wonderful tailors who have invented a special way of weaving a cloth so light and fine that it can't be seen by anyone who is too stupid to appreciate it," they told the guard.

The guard sent for the court chamberlain, the chamberlain notified the prime minister, and the prime minister ran to the emperor with the incredible news. The emperor, consumed by curiosity, decided to see the two scoundrels.

"Your Majesty, besides being invisible, this cloth will be woven in colors and patterns especially for you," said the wily tailors.

The emperor gave the two men a bag of gold in exchange for their promise to begin work immediately.

The tailors asked for a loom and a quantity of silk and gold thread, and pretended to set to work. The emperor thought his money well spent. Not only would he get a new suit, he would find out which of his subjects were stupid!

A few days later, he called in the prime minister, a man known for his common sense, and said, "Go and see how the work is getting on."

"We're almost finished," said the two scoundrels, welcoming the prime minister. "Just look at these colors, and feel the softness of the material!"

The old man bent over the loom. "I can't see a thing," he said to himself. "That must mean I'm stupid!" He coughed nervously. "Ahem! What a marvelous fabric! I shall certainly tell the emperor."

The two scoundrels rubbed their hands gleefully, and requested more golden thread. Before long, they arrived at the royal apartments, ready to take measurements for the new suit.

"Come in, come in," said the emperor eagerly.

The scoundrels bowed low and pretended to stagger under the weight of the cloth. "Here it is, Your Majesty. What do you think of it? Just look at the rich colors and feel how soft it is!"

Of course the emperor could see and feel nothing. "I must be stupid!" he thought in a panic. "I'd better pretend to see it so no one will know." And so he praised the beautiful cloth, unaware that everyone around him was thinking the very same thing about themselves!

The two scoundrels took the emperor's measurements. They set to work, busily cutting the air with scissors and stitching together pieces of nothing at all.

After a while, they said, "Your Majesty, you'll have to take off your clothes to try on your new suit." They draped the invisible garments about him and held up a mirror.

The emperor was dreadfully embarrassed, but as the bystanders seemed to notice nothing amiss, he felt relieved. "Yes—ahhh hmmm—a beautiful suit," he declared.

"Your Majesty," said the prime minister, "the people are anxious to see this amazing fabric and to admire your new suit." The emperor was doubtful about showing himself naked to his subjects. "Oh well," he comforted himself, "only the stupid ones will know."

"All right," he said grandly. "I will grant the people's wish." He summoned his open carriage and a stately procession was formed. In front walked the court officials, anxiously scrutinizing the faces in the street.

All the people had gathered in the main square to get a better look, and to find out how stupid their neighbors might be. Strangely enough, as the emperor passed, a murmur of admiration arose from the crowd.

"Look at the emperor's new clothes. How fine they are!" They all tried to conceal their disappointment and dismay at not seeing the clothes.

By and by, however, a child ran up to the carriage. He had no important job to protect and was only able to judge by the evidence of his own eyes.

"Why, the emperor is naked!" he blurted out.

"Fool!" his father scolded, dragging the child away.

But the boy's remark had been overheard, and was repeated again and again until everyone shouted, "The boy is right. The emperor is naked!"

The emperor realized to his shame that the people were right, but thought it better to continue the procession and pretend that anyone who couldn't see his clothes was stupid. And so he stood stiffly in his carriage all the way home, resolving never to be vain again.

As for the two scoundrels, they made off with the gold and all the precious thread, laughing all the way.

THE GOLDEN FISH

Once upon a time there was a poor fisherman who lived in a humble cottage near the sea. One day, he set off as usual with his load of nets to go fishing.

"Don't dare come home empty-handed!" shouted his nagging wife.

Down on the shore, he stood on a rock and threw his net into the sea. Something shiny caught his eye.

"What a strange fish!" he muttered, picking up a golden form from the net. His amazement grew when he heard the fish speak.

"Kind fisherman, let me go! I am the son of the Sea King, and if you free me I will grant any wish you care to make!"

Alarmed, the fisherman tossed the fish back into the water. But when he reached home his wife scolded him soundly.

"You should have asked for something. Go back to the beach and wish for a new washtub. Just look at the state of our old thing!"

The poor man went back to the rock. As soon as he called the fish, it popped its head out of the water.

"Were you calling me?"

The fisherman explained what his wife wanted.

"You were good to me," replied the fish. "Go home and you'll find your wish has come true."

Certain that his wife would be pleased, the fisherman hurried home. But the minute he opened the door, his wife screeched, "So it really is a magic fish! You can't possibly be content with a miserable washtub. Go straight back and wish for a new house!"

The fisherman hurried back to the shore. "I wonder if the fish will come again?" he muttered. "Little fish! Little fish!" he called from the water's edge.

"Here I am! What do you want this time?" he heard it ask.

"Well, my wife would like—"

"I can imagine!" remarked the fish. "What does she want now?"

"A big house," stammered the fisherman.

"All right! Since you were kind to me, you shall have your wish!" The fisherman lingered on the way home, enjoying the feeling of making his wife happy. But as he caught sight of the roof of the splendid new house, his wife rushed up to him in a fury.

"Look here! Now that we know how powerful this fish is, we can't be content with a mere house. Run back and ask for a real palace! And fine clothes! And jewels, too!"

This request upset the fisherman greatly. However, he had been henpecked for so many years that he couldn't say no.

He trudged back to the water's edge. Full of doubt, he stood on the rock and called the little fish, but the sea began to get very rough. Quite some time passed before the fish leapt from the waves.

"I'm sorry to trouble you again," said the fisherman, much embarrassed. "My wife has had second thoughts. She'd like a palace, and fine clothes and jewels as well."

Again the fish granted the fisherman's wishes, but it seemed less friendly than before. The fisherman turned homeward, relieved to have his wife's demands satisfied.

What a magnificent place home was! At the top of a flight of steps stood his wife, dressed like a great lady and dripping in jewels.

"Go back and ask for—" she began impatiently. But the fisherman interrupted her.

"What? With such a fine palace! We must be content with what we have. Don't you think you're asking too much?"

"Do as you're told," snapped the wife. "Ask the fish to make me an Empress!"

The poor fisherman set off unhappily for the seashore. A storm had blown up, and terrible flashes of lightning lit up the black sky. Kneeling on the rock amid the spray, the fisherman called to the little fish.

When it came, he told of his wife's latest demand. But this time, after listening in silence, the golden fish disappeared beneath the waves without saying a word.

A great flash of lightning shot through the sky, and the fisherman saw that the palace had vanished without a trace. The humble cottage stood where it had always been.

His wife was waiting for him in tears.

"It serves you right!" grumbled the fisherman. Deep in his heart, however, he was glad that everything had returned to normal.

Each day after that he went fishing, but never again did he see the golden fish.

THE BOOK OF SPELLS

Once upon a time, there lived an ogre in the middle of a forest. He was big, cruel, and heartless, but he liked his house to be tidy.

"I'm always out hunting, fishing, and causing trouble," he said to himself one day. "I need someone to look after the house, clean the floors, and wash the laundry every week." And off he went to some poor peasants' houses scattered around the forest edge.

The ogre crouched down beside one of the cottages. Soon, a boy and a girl came out. The ogre stretched out his big hand and grabbed them.

"You'll be my servants," he said as he carried them off. "I'll feed you, but beware: if you try to run away, you'll be the next dish!"

The terrified children lived in the ogre's house for a long time. Each evening the ogre would pull out a large book and study it carefully.

"It must be a Book of Spells," the clever children whispered to each other. They waited until the ogre went away, and began to read the book and learn the spells.

"Sister, I think I know enough now. Let's run away!"

"Oh! Are you sure you know how to cast spells?" asked the girl anxiously.

"Of course!" said he. "Come on, before the ogre gets back!" Off the pair ran into the forest.

"I hear somebody running!" cried the girl suddenly. It was the ogre, and with his long legs he would surely catch up with them soon.

"Don't worry. I'll cast a spell!" said the boy. And so saying, he turned himself into a pond and his sister into a minnow! A moment later, the ogre rushed up and saw what had happened.

"If only I had a fishing line," he growled, and ran off to fetch one.

The children returned to their own forms and fled through the forest, but the ogre was soon on their heels. He was just about to grab them when the boy cast a second spell, turning himself into a shrine and his sister into an angel painted on the wall.

The ogre would have loved to kick the shrine to bits, but he didn't dare. "I'll burn you down instead!" he shouted, and ran off for a bundle of firewood.

In the meantime, however, the children had taken to their heels once more. They ran until they were exhausted and could feel the ogre's hot breath behind them. On the point of being snatched, the boy cast a third spell, changing himself and his sister into grains of corn mingled with thousands of others on the threshing floor.

"Hah! You think you can beat me with my own spells, do you? I'm far more cunning than you!" the ogre roared, and promptly changed himself into a cockerel that started pecking all the grains of corn. It seemed as though the children would never escape now, but just as the ogre was about to peck him, the boy turned into a fox, pounced on the cockerel, and gobbled it up!

Thankfully, the two children made their way to the edge of the forest safe and sound, never again to fear the ogre.

THE HARE AND THE ELEPHANT

In the jungles of India there once lived a young elephant whose playmate was a very big hare.

One day the hare said to the elephant, "Who is bigger, you or me?"

The little elephant nearly choked on his banana. "Why, you're not as high as my knee!"

"So you say," retorted the hare. "We need a judge, don't you agree?"

"All right," replied the elephant, somewhat taken aback.

"Let's go to the village and see what the humans have to say," suggested the hare. As they neared the village, they met some people. "Look at that young elephant! Isn't he small?" remarked one. "Yes indeed," said another, "but he'll soon grow up."

The hare paraded in front of the elephant, his chest puffed out.

"What a huge hare!" cried the villagers.

The hare turned to his friend. "We can go home now. That settles it. I'm huge and you're small."

The young elephant tossed his great head, too exasperated to speak. But back on the jungle path, he finally lifted his foot and said to the hare, who was strutting ahead, "Get out of my way, big hare, before a small elephant crushes you!"